David Next Door

Written by Melanie L. Babendreier

Illustrated by Amy Bates

David leans to the side when he walks.

He waves and cries wild bird sounds behind his fence.

I hear him when I play ball on the back lawn.

I watch David from my bedroom window.

He pulls leaves from the oak tree in his yard.

His fingers are long and busy.

What is he trying to do? Is he playing a secret game?

David doesn't go to my school.

He doesn't ride a bike or play outside his yard.

I don't understand him. Why is he so different?

David's mother plays ball with him.

She talks to him with her hands.

David chases the ball, smiling.

He's always smiling.

I don't know why.

Sometimes David and his dad walk by my house.

They hold hands and point at things.

David looks at my house and my yard.

I wonder what he's thinking.

When David rides in the car,

he presses his nose against the window.

I wonder what he sees.

I wonder where they go.

I ask my mother why David is different.

She tells me something happened before David was born.

She says he needs a friend.

How can I be his friend?

David can't even hear me say hello.

One day I throw my ball too hard.

It bounces into David's yard.

I look through the fence. I can't see it anywhere.

The next day David's gate is open.

His dog barks and his mother looks.

Where is David?

I am in my tree house.

I hear birds, and I hear something else.

I look down through tangled leaves.

David is crying under my tree.

I don't like David to cry.

I climb down.

"What's wrong?

Why are you crying?"

David looks at me

and sings a soft asking song.

He holds out his hand.

His fingers curve around my ball.

Slowly he puts it into my hand.

David waits for me to show him the way home.

He smiles at me.

I smile back and take his hand.

Then he sings a happy song, a wild bird song without words.